LOVE SPELLS

A Novella

LINDA CASEBEER

SEREALITIES PRESS
www.serealities.com

ISBN: 0615923690
ISBN 13: 9780615923697

Library of Congress Control Number: 2013922899
Serealities Press, Birmingham, Alabama

Acknowledgements

The author wishes to thank Holly Aasen and Kim Sloan for their contributions to the manuscript, and Edwin Casebeer for his careful reading and feedback.

One

There was a girl. For the past three years, she had been locked up. If she went twenty feet away from the cottage where she lived, she was called a runner. Like the girl with the dragon tattoo, someday she planned to get even with the people who had put her there, the people who had made her a ward of the court. She had learned how to shoot a gun when she was twelve, and she had ideas. In three days, they would have to let her go, on her eighteenth birthday. She was desperate to get out. All week, she had hardly been able to breathe. She couldn't sleep. No matter what, she would not be locked up again. She had no job. No social security card. No birth certificate. No photo ID. No high school diploma. She had no place to live yet. She was a beautiful blue-eyed redhead. Her plan was to move in with one of the men she had met online. Unfortunately for her story, men would always be looking for a girl like her, and she would always be looking for true love.

For as long as she could remember, other people had decided where she would live. Caseworkers. Advocates. Judges. She couldn't remember the first time she was put into the system. They told her it was the usual story. Her mother's boyfriend yelling, beating up her mother and waving a gun around, the neighbors calling child welfare, child welfare taking her and her sister away in the middle of the night. After months, back with her mother, then sent to her father and his girlfriend. Her father getting drunk and hitting her. More foster care. Finally the orphanage, except that they didn't call it that. In three days the system wouldn't want her anymore. Which was fine with her.

She was so tired of this place. She wanted them to stop making her get up and go to chapel every morning. Not everything was about God. She didn't want the pills they gave her. The pills made her sleepy. She thought they made her take those pills to keep her quiet. So she would behave. Sometimes she got really mad at everybody. They said she had ADHD. Depression. They said she was bipolar like her mother. Nobody had ever proved that. She figured the only thing crazy about her was what came from being locked up.

When she left, they would give her the money she made working at the Canteen. But she hadn't figured out how to get more. She had already put her clothes in the small bag they had given her for packing. And a cardboard box for what else was left. She just needed somebody to sign her out and pick her up. When she got out, she wanted to be tough. While other girls were watching *Twilight,* she was watching *The Girl.* Three movies, the ones made in Sweden. Her aunt had given her the DVDs and a small DVD player on her birthday a year ago. She had never seen movies with subtitles before. She didn't even mind the subtitles. She watched them over and over again. She knew the movies by heart. She knew how Lisbeth, the Girl, dressed so people would leave her alone. Most of her own clothes were black, what clothes she had. She wanted to dye her hair black. She knew Lisbeth's hair was red underneath.

She wanted a tattoo. In her mind, she could see what she wanted. A wasp on her neck like Lisbeth. She wanted angel wings on her shoulders because her mother had named her Angelique. Her mother had been a churchgoer then. She remembers her mother saying *"Trust Jesus"* a lot. But her mother couldn't just name her Angel or Angela. The name had to be fancy. Angelique sounded pretty when she was little. When she was locked up, they called her Geli and a lot of other things like Geli Bean and Geli Roll. She wanted to be tougher. She wanted more piercings. Only her ears were pierced. Her roommate Jenny had used an ice cube to numb her ears, jammed a needle through each ear lobe and stuck in some of her old rhinestone earrings. The holes had gotten infected. Her roommate had said her ears were weeping.

Two

There were seven other girls in her cottage. Each one was her own story. Most of the girls had grown up around there. The ways they got there were mostly the same. Meth labs. Guns. Mothers who were addicts. Off and on boyfriends with no patience for kids. Fathers that drank or beat them or both. Courts. Judges. The stories went around in circles. As soon as one girl left the cottage, another one got referred. When they left the cottage, the girls wanted to be loved. A lot of them ended up pregnant. In chapel they preached abstinence, and *"Never kill a baby."*

At the moment she was the oldest girl in the cottage. Her roommate, Jenny, said she was very mad that Angelique was leaving first. Jenny's mother was supposed to come and take her home. That was always the story. Jenny wasn't talking to Angelique she was so mad. They had been roommates for more than a year. Angelique and Jenny were from the same town. It was about an hour away. Nothing happened anymore in that town. The school was closed. The factory was closed. There was only one store. Feed and seed. A bar. There were two churches. Both of of them had graveyards. Jenny's mother hadn't had a job since the factory closed. Nobody knew where her father had gone. Jenny had a brother who was too old to be in the system. He said he was going to volunteer for the army and get a bonus if he passed the physical. The bonus would be more money than anybody he knew had ever seen. He said the same thing about enlisting every time he came. Jenny told Angela she thought he was stealing something. Maybe car parts. Maybe copper. She wasn't sure what. Sometimes he had money in his pocket.

Angelique's mother never came to visit her anymore. She hadn't seen her for more than three years. Jenny's mother and her grandmother came on visiting days, every third Saturday. Once in a while with her brother. He was blonde like Jenny. Handsome. Jenny's grandmother would just sit there shaking her head a lot. Talked about everything Jenny's mother was addicted to. Said she would take Jenny home with her but she had to take care of Jenny's grandfather. Jenny's mother just stared off somewhere Jenny couldn't see. Sometimes Jenny yelled at her mother. Pounded her fists on her mother's chest. Jenny got detention points for that. Jenny's mother didn't say anything. Just sat there. Her grandmother told Jenny to be respectful. Jenny said she just wanted to go home. At least Jenny had a mother to yell at.

Angelique hardly ever had visitors. Her father had come twice the past year. Each time with a different girlfriend. On visiting days there were no activities. All of the girls stayed most of the day in the big room of the cottage. The ones who didn't have visitors sat around and braided each other's hair in small braids tight to the scalp. Cornrows. Prison hair. Angelique had so much hair it was always hard for anybody to braid. Her thick red curls went all directions. The girls pulled so tight it gave her a headache every time.

If her mother had ever come to visit she would have told everybody Angelique had her mother's blue eyes. *"The blue of blue-eyed grass that only blooms for a week in the spring,"* her useless mother used to sing, sort of, on her sentimental drunk days. But most of her drinking days, her mother had just screamed at her. Her mother thought she would write country western songs and get rich. Probably still thought so. Her aunt thought her mother had gone to Nashville when she disappeared three years ago.

None of the other girls would be able to leave when Angelique did. First, she thought she would promise to come back and see them. Bring them Cheetos. Send them money. Write to them. The sign by the side of the chapel door said that the door had been open since 1850 for the most deserted children. The rich man who started the place probably thought he was doing something good. All

Christian and charity. That was a long time ago. It had turned into people paid by the state to take in kids. Kids too old to be placed. She would never forget the other girls. Especially Jenny. But when she really thought about it, she knew she would not come back. She knew that when she was picked up for the last time she would be gone. It made her shiver to think about it.

Three

Getting somebody to pick her up and sign for her, that is where it could get tricky, she thought. She had decided she would not leave with her father. She had written almost every day to her aunt to ask her to come and pick her up on the first day of the month. Her aunt always remembered her birthday. She had called her aunt last week. Her aunt said she would come if she could get off work. She had made her aunt promise. Angelique didn't want to stay with her. Her aunt only had a room in a garage, and worked all the time anyway. Double shifts when she could. But if a boyfriend showed up to pick her up she knew that could be a problem. All she wanted was to leave and really nobody could stop her. They wanted to get rid of her. For years people had said Angelique would be thankful some day for being there. For the discipline. Not Angelique.

So the discipline was like this. She was locked up. Told what to do every day from six o'clock in the morning until nine at night. Everything in groups. Breakfast. Chapel. School. Therapy. Exercise. Dinner. Shower. They would chase her if she ran away from the cottage. She could go sit on the swings or on the bench outside even when it was really cold. Sometimes one of the teachers would take her to power walk. But there was no way out. Except for the girl who hid in the laundry truck and was brought back that night. And the one who killed herself. It was a girl from her cottage. She would never forget that day. Nothing moved. Air. Sound. The ambulance came. No siren. There was blood everywhere on the floor of the shower, where her body had crumpled. That night they had sent the girls from her cottage to sleep on the floor in the gym on exercise mats. The next day the shower was cleaned up. Nobody wanted to go back to the cottage, but there was nowhere else to go.

Four

Her father and his latest girlfriend, Rhonda, had come on her last visiting day. Angelique thought the caseworker had called him to come. She hadn't seen her father for a long time. His eyes were red. He smelled like beer. He had a baseball cap pulled down over his face. He let Rhonda do the talking. Angelique couldn't exactly figure Rhonda out, how Rhonda ended up with her father. It sounded like Rhonda had just wandered into town. Angelique knew her father lived on a disability check so it wasn't like he had a lot of money. Or was handsome. So she didn't know what Rhonda saw in him. Still, she didn't think he had hit Rhonda. Yet. She didn't see any marks on her face. Or her arms. That day, the weather had been warm for May and Rhonda had worn a yellow sundress, not like she was trying to hide something. Rhonda had worn a wooden cross around her neck. It had reminded Angelique of something when she was little. When her mother wore the locket with a picture of Jesus and wouldn't take it off, even to take a bath, until the chain had started to turn her neck green.

Rhonda had said she wanted Angelique to come and live with them. That she went to church every Sunday but Angelique's father wouldn't ever go with her, so it would be nice to have some company. She walked all the way to church every Sunday and back. She hadn't seemed to mind, said it made her peaceful to walk. "Sometimes it's better just to have to have a roof over your head," Rhonda said.

Angelique had told her father and Rhonda she didn't need a place to live. She had told them she had her own plan. She was going to move in with her boyfriend. She didn't tell them she hadn't decided which of the men she had met online was her boyfriend. Rhonda had told her she had plenty of time for boyfriends. She had told Angelique she was beautiful, that men would always want her, and that was the problem. She remembered the way Rhonda had touched her hair when she said it.

"Just think about it a little, Angelique, we could plant a garden," Rhonda had said. She had some tomato seeds that should have been planted in April. If they had enough faith the seeds would grow tomatoes before it got too cold. Then Rhonda and her father had left. Her father hadn't said anything.

Five

Months ago Angelique had started thinking about her birthday. It wasn't like anybody had promised a cake. Or a party. Angelique knew the story. It was time for her to leave. What they really meant was they wouldn't get paid to take care of her anymore.

Jenny already knew who was coming next, the new roommate. A referral named Janet. They didn't let time go by when they weren't getting money for a bed. Angelique did want to leave. Jenny was right about that. Who wouldn't? A free pass out the front door. And when she left, she wanted a real boyfriend. She had been locked up long enough, and nobody was going to tell her what to do anymore. She would be telling them.

Cottages were separate but the girls had been allowed to mix with the boys at times. Most of the boys in there had been in a lot of trouble. It's how they got there. It wasn't like they had killed anybody. But they were messed up, one way or another. She wanted to have a boyfriend who loved her, and she wanted to live with him, somebody who had his own place. A job. A car. And some money. Where he would take care of her and love her forever.

It wasn't like she was a virgin. It was one of the older boys. Nobody else knew. He wasn't around long. But she had loved him. He had dark curly hair she could run her fingers through. He played soccer. Except nobody played soccer there. One day a cousin had come to claim him. To take him to a farm to work.

Said he was as strong as two of the men he had hired. She didn't know where he lived. Or have any idea how to find him when she got out. More than anything now she wanted a new boyfriend who wasn't going to leave her. Jenny had told her if she would go on Facebook or MeetMe or Match.com, she could find boyfriends who would want to marry her. Her brother had told her about it. It's where he found girlfriends.

She needed a boyfriend. The last thing she wanted to do was live with her father. She was sure that he didn't want her to come home either. He had been putting on a show. Besides, he was the reason she had been locked up. So why would she go back to that? People said they were a lot alike. That's why they got into fights. He would get so mad at her. He would tell her what to do all the time. And she wouldn't. Then he would get madder. And he would get drunk. Then he would hit her. Everybody knew it. The caseworkers knew it. That's why she hated them. Her father wouldn't say he had hit her. His lawyer told him not to. So they had made her a ward of the court and locked her up.

Six

Angelique had watched over and over again in the movies how the girl with the dragon tattoo did what she did. It was computers that got Lisbeth somewhere. Angelique wanted to be like that. To get even. To get things to happen the way she wanted them to. But if computers were the answer, that was a problem. To begin with, they weren't allowed to have phones, and where would she get one anyway. They could call home once a week from the phone in the hall, but that wasn't getting her online. The computers they used for school were old, but her only chance. At first she hadn't thought she would be able to figure it out. How to get on to Facebook. And the dating sites. She tried some things when people weren't looking. Nothing worked. Sites were blocked.

Then Jenny's older brother came one Saturday. He knew something about computers and phones. He took her out by the swings where people couldn't hear. He used his phone to set up accounts for her. Told her to use an alias. The name he gave her was Betty Boop. It was what his grandmother had named her cat. He thought it was funny. He took her photo and sent a copy to one of her new accounts. He told her enough to get her started. He told her how to get around the firewall. When he was finished, he called her Betty Boop. Kissed her hard on the lips. Laughed. And left.

Later that week when she was supposed to be doing homework, she made it past the firewall. She knew what she wanted from a man. She had thought a lot about it. That part was easy. Then she waited to see what would happen.

She needed to be careful. One of the teachers in the library had checked something on the computers and started yelling at all of them. As long as it wasn't her name, nobody knew. Finally, the teacher had let them back into the library.

After that first week, men had been talking to her online. Then it was easy. Flirting with them. She knew her photo looked good. She had lied to her father and Rhonda. There were more than ten men who wanted her to move in, not just one boyfriend. They were all promising something. Red roses. Concerts. Presents. A trip to Disney World. "Why not Paris?" she asked. He told her there was an Eiffel Tower in Disney. She would leave one message, and another would show up. She could be happy just reading them.

She couldn't believe how many men matched her profile. Some were creepy. She wasn't stupid. She had not answered the ones who had asked her what she was wearing when she went to bed. Or about sexual positions. Or who had not put their pictures up. Or would not say where they were living. Could be jail for all she knew. For now she had narrowed it down to three. As Jenny would say, here was the deal. One was her age and lived up the road in the Community. His name was Andrew. Two was Brian. Brian had been married before and had two children. He was always fighting with his ex-wife. He wanted to get married and start over. And then there was Chuck. He had said he would take her places she hadn't been like Disney World. She called the men the ABCs.

Seven

Andrew had asked her if she had freckles. Most of them asked. It was her red hair, and they couldn't really tell from her photo. When she had told him no, he called her Freckles anyway. She called him No Freckles. She had liked him. The problem was he didn't have a car. He told her that right away. But he told her he knew somebody who did. They only had horses on the farm. She was used to seeing the horses and buggies in town. He had to decide if he would be baptized in the church. Told her no way he was going back. All his life he had lived there. On the farm. People had told him what to do. Not him. He had already decided. He figured he could fish and get a job doing carpentry. He was in love with her picture. He and his buddy had found a fishing cabin on the lake that nobody had lived in for a long time. He was living with his buddy. He wanted her to come and live with them. They would catch fish every day. Even in winter they could ice fish. He said he would take care of her. And he said he loved her.

Brian complained about his ex-wife and said Angelique was so much prettier. Called her Darlin' over and over again. He talked about his kids. How hard it was to get them to school before he had to go to work every day. About his son who was going crazy through the divorce. He said he couldn't wait for her to come live with him. He had plans. For all of them. They could get married next month when everything was final. She could be a stay at home mom and he would take care of her. He made good money. He had a new car. He just needed a wife to make a family.

Or the Disney World guy, Chuck. He was thirty. She had never had a boy-friend with a beard. He had his own house out in the woods. He told her she was beautiful, that he was especially partial to redheads. That she could come any time and live with him. She was just the woman he was looking for. He said he made deliveries to Florida. He would take her when he was going that way. Out for a good time he said. He had said she sounded like she could use a good time. She hadn't told him that she had been locked up for three years, that he was more right than he knew. He didn't say exactly what he was delivering but it was probably drugs that sounded better than the ones she was taking. Going places sounded good too. She hadn't been anywhere outside of two counties ever.

They had sent messages. She had sent messages back. Most days she had been able to use the computer. It had seemed like a long time ago since Jenny's brother had shown her how to get online. A lot had happened since then. More than ever now, she wanted out. She had everything packed in the bag or the box. Two more days to wait. Long boring hot days, and the days were getting hotter. She was still worried about getting picked up. She didn't know what would hap-pen if her aunt didn't show up.

Eight

S he started to doubt her plan. She wondered what would happen if her aunt
wouldn't drop her off where she wanted to go. Her aunt had opinions about
things. Let her know it too. Just in case, she decided to send Ashley a message on
Facebook. Ashley had been her best friend since she was seven. She hadn't seen
her for a long time. Ashley had lived next door when Angelique had lived with
her mother for a while. And once before, she had run away from a foster home
to Ashley's house. Ashley's mother had found her taking a shower one morning
and gotten mad. Started yelling at her, said she had to call the authorities. And
she did. Just because of a shower. But that was a long time ago.

Maybe Ashley's mother wouldn't mind so much this time. If she couldn't
convince her aunt to take her to see the man she wanted, then maybe her aunt
would take her to Ashley's house. She could get a ride from there. She hadn't
known Ashley had had a baby until she found her on Facebook. Lots of baby
pictures. The main picture of Ashley on her site wasn't Ashley. It was the baby.
Ashley had named her Penelope Ann. Instead of saying Ashley, it said Penelope
Ann's mom. In her message to Ashley, she told her she was getting out. That she
wanted to come and see her. Wanted to see Penelope Ann. She thought that was
what Ashley would want to hear.

On Sunday she had gone to church like she did every Sunday. Afterwards she
had sneaked into the library. The door wasn't locked. She had left the lights off.
Every one of the men she was flirting with had left her some kind of message.

She had found the one she was looking for from Ashley. Ashley had said her mom was about to throw her out. The baby cried too much. It was hurting her business. People who came to her for love spells didn't want to hear a baby crying in the background. Her mother kept telling her she needed to get her own place. Or help her with the business.

Ashley's mother was the Lovely Louise of Lovely Louise's Love Spells. Ever since they were growing up, Louise had wanted Ashley to join her in the business. Ashley was fourth generation. When they were growing up and Angelique hadn't understood *fourth generation*, Ashley had told her that meant great-grandmother, grandmother, mother, daughter. *The gift,* she had said. Ashley's mother had wanted her to be the next one. But Ashley had never wanted anything to do with spells. Louise was known all over the state for her spells. Other people asked for spells for money or jobs or other things. But people only came to Ashley's mother for love spells. She had a sign out in front of her house with a sweeping heart. There were all kinds of stories about her powers, her spells that had worked. She claimed she could produce passion and lust, bring back lovers, get lovers to propose, or stop divorces.

And lately, according to Ashley, Louise's internet business had been growing. She even had a Visa and Mastercard setup to take donations. Some days, Ashley said, Louise had more messages than she could manage. And apparently Louise and Ashley were fighting since she kept telling Ashley that she was of age, and she could begin to take on the work. But Angelique remembered that Ashley had always been stubborn about it. She had said she didn't believe any of it. She had watched her mother for years, and she had insisted it was all a scam. Witchcraft. Candles. That you couldn't just demand something and get it because you wanted it to happen. *What about the other person,* Ashley used to say. *Don't they have anything to say about it?*

Ashley told Angelique that she was trying to get a real job. She had tried getting a job at the new Kroger store in the produce department, but there hadn't been anybody to take care of the baby. Maybe Angelique would take care of the baby for her so she could earn some money and get out of her mother's place. There was no room there anyway. At least she had a mother to fight with, even if it was Lovely Louise.

That night it was still hot. Jenny wouldn't talk to her. She was curled up reading. Jenny read until she fell asleep every night. Angelique couldn't sleep. No breeze. She lay there sweating. Staring at the ceiling. Looking at the full moon through the window. They said the full moon made people crazy. Maybe it was a sign. Her birthday moon. Maybe she was crazy. Maybe it was everybody else. She was so tired, but she couldn't sleep. She never dreamed anymore. She thought it was the pills. She used to dream in color, almost like a movie. She used to see her sister and her mother in her dreams. One time they drove off the end of the road, a blue road that didn't go anywhere. The road just ended and they were gone. She knew one thing for sure. Her mother wasn't coming to get her. Instead, the flirting men's messages ran through her head. The photos. The places they said they lived. Where she could live too.

Nine

Then it was ten o'clock on the morning of her birthday and she had come to the office. This was it. She had tried to say goodbye to Jenny. And the others. She had gone back to the cottage to get her things after chapel and the breakfast she had not eaten. Jenny had picked up a book and had thrown it at her. Angelique had turned away and had said thank you to the housemother who had never been a mother. She had known she was supposed to. She had taken her bag and her box and walked out.

The caseworker was waiting for her. She had sent a message to Andrew that she would like to shoot the caseworkers and asked him if he had a gun at his cabin.

"Like my mother says, you have other fish to fry. Just come to the lake," he had replied.

The caseworker told her to sit down. She told her to be careful with her money, to be careful around people she didn't know, that the world was full of people who would try to take advantage of her. Angelique just looked down at the floor and waited for her to finish. She gave Angelique a prescription for the pills they had been giving her and told her where to go to get it. She told her about the free clinic for birth control.

But no one had come to pick her up. Her aunt knew the first day of the month was her birthday. Maybe her car wouldn't start. Maybe she couldn't get off work. The caseworker was tapping her pen on the desk. Said she has another appointment in an hour on the other side of the county and couldn't wait around all day. Said the temperature was already ninety degrees. Then she asked the woman in the office for a glass of water. More pen tapping. "Why can't people just do what they are supposed to?"

With the glass of water came Rhonda. Breathless. Sweat on her forehead. "Your dad is waiting in the car. He told me to help with your things." Now Angelique could feel her face get hot. Right up to the top of her head. She didn't think she had ever been that mad at anybody. The caseworker's name was Rebecca, but they called her the Old Bag since she was older than the others and had bags under her eyes. This was the Old Bag's fault. She had done this. She made it sound like her father could just stop in and take her away. Angelique said she was not going to live with her father. She wasn't going to school anymore. She said she had her own people. She started in on how mean her father had been to her. That Rebecca didn't know anything. Then she picked up the glass of water on the table next to Rebecca and threw it at her. Water soaked the front of her mulberry colored blouse. Dripped down on the signed paper in front of her. "You are in trouble now, Missy," she said.

Angelique said, "So arrest me. You can't give me detention points or anything. So what? You don't want me to stay here. I can't stay here. And I'm not going with her. With him. Ever. You can't make me."

"So if you are not going with your father, Missy, what are you going to do?"

More screaming from Angelique. A security guard came to the door. The woman in the office had called him. Rebecca and Angelique glared at each other across the desk. Rhonda just stood there.

"Now look here," Rebecca said to her. "You don't have any other way to leave." The Old Bag started going on about diplomas and how Angelique would never get a job without one. How did she think she was going to eat? Where would she find a roof over her head?

"Her Aunt Lily called and said *Sorry Sorry Sorry* about a million times on the phone," the woman from the office came in to tell them. "She said they wouldn't let her off work. Another woman on the shift called in sick. She had to finish the shift. But she would be there at four o'clock to pick up her niece."

Rebecca raised her voice again, saying she was late for another meeting. The woman in the office told Rebecca to go on, that the office would take care of the paperwork in the afternoon when the aunt got there. Angelique was told she could wait in the library if she thought she could be respectful and quiet. The woman in the office would let her know when her aunt came and would sign her out. Rhonda looked like she didn't know what to do next. The woman in the office told Rhonda she could go. And Rhonda backed out of the door.

Ten

Angelique headed for the library. She could still feel the heat in her face and her stomach clenching. Her aunt hadn't come to visit for a while. She had come every Christmas. And Easter. Sometimes she signed her out for a weekend. But that hadn't happened for a long time. Every time her aunt had come, she would say she felt guilty that she hadn't gotten custody of Angelique. It was her sister after all who had left Angelique. Her aunt would tell her she felt horrible that her mother had run away. And taken Angelique's sister Brittany with her. Angelique knew her mother always liked Brittany better anyway. Brittany was the smart one. Her mother had said Brittany would go to Princeton one day.

Her mother and Brittany had come to see her one time at the beginning. They had brought her brownies. Her mother said she had baked something special into the brownies that would make her feel good. She kept saying *feel so gooooood*. They had sat with her for a while. Her mother had showed her how to take some blue yarn from the craft bin and a crochet hook and make a long string of loops. She had said the loops could be a scarf. Or an afghan. Or anything she wanted it to be. Then they were gone. The housemother had put the brownies away, and she had never seen them again.

The next thing she had heard of her mother was her aunt telling her that her mother had to run away this time. Across state lines. She thought she might have gone to Nashville. For the songs. "Maybe she will get lucky and we'll see her on stage someday," she would say. Her mother was running away because she and Brittany had been living with a boyfriend who had a meth lab. She kept saying the boyfriend took good care of them. But she was about to be arrested. Brittany would be taken away. So she took off with her. Her aunt said nobody had seen her since.

Aunt Lily was the pretty one. Prettier than her mother. Everybody said so. Aunt Lily's hair was a color people called caramel. Her hair was straight and swung around her face when she turned. Her mother had the same thick red curls as Angelique. But her mother's face was more like an owl or something. Maybe it was the glasses. The two women had the same mother but different fathers.

Aunt Lily had gotten married right out of high school. She had married a man ten years older than she was. He owned the liquor stores in two towns. He told her they would always have a steady income. They had a nice brick house close to the lake. They liked to go fishing together on Sundays. She had wished she could have children. It was something about scar tissue. She said her sister was so lucky that way. She could just pop out those babies with no trouble. She liked watching her nieces growing up. She would buy them gifts at Christmas and on their birthdays.

Angelique knew things had changed for her aunt when somebody stuck a gun in her husband's face to rob him at the liquor store late one night. The robber had not ever been caught. It wasn't about the money. Her husband had kept a gun under the counter but had not gotten to it in time. The way her aunt told the story, after that her husband had bought more guns. He had started going to the shooting range. He had decided to practice more. That was when Angelique learned to shoot. He had taken her to the shooting range with him. It was before she had been locked up. After the robbery, it seemed like that was all he thought about, guns and hunting deer and ducks. He couldn't wait for the seasons to open. He had a deer head stuffed to put over the mantel, then a second deer head because the antlers were so good. They had to move the first one over so they could hang two there. He had hired somebody to run the liquor stores and only went to collect his money once a week.

One night after he had been drinking, he had gone a little crazy. He had tried to kill Aunt Lily. At least he had stuck a gun in her face the same way the robber had. He wanted her to see what was bothering him. She had called the police. He kept yelling he would never hurt her. But that had been it for her. She wasn't staying around to see what would happen next. She had gone and gotten herself a job at the factory that made flags. U.S. flags. State flags. And banners for rich people to put on poles outside their houses that looked like spring with butterflies and Easter eggs. Or turkeys for Thanksgiving.

She had rented a room she called an apartment that had been somebody's garage. She had a routine now, mostly working. Sometimes she worked double shifts at the factory. On Friday night she would go with her friend from work to drink Mai Tais with little umbrellas. On Saturdays she always went to the library. She read all the time when she wasn't at work, mostly murder mysteries. On Sundays, she would go to church. She said it was what her mama taught her to do on Sunday.

Eleven

Her aunt had always worried about her nieces. She didn't know which was worse, the niece who was with her mother while her mother was running away, or the one that had gotten locked up. And always, she was sorry. Sorry. Sorry that she didn't get Angelique and bring her home to live with her. It was all at the same time as her troubles started. The robbery. The guns. Sorry her husband had taught Angelique to shoot.

Her aunt had never lived by herself. It was enough to figure out where to go and what to do. So she came to see Angelique when she was locked up. Her aunt would tell anybody those girls were both the sweetest girls growing up. What good hearts they had. Especially with all they had been through. Their mother, though, could be a horror. Their mother would bounce around from one man to another. Even after the girls were taken away the first time and were put in foster care. Their mother had been pregnant two more times after that. One a bloody miscarriage. The last one had been born when their mother was between boyfriends. Nowhere to live. No money. No way to take care of another child. The last one had been given up for adoption. Her mother kept thinking the girl would come looking for her birth mother when she grew up. "Blue eyes like me," she would say.

Angelique hadn't expected her aunt to take her in this time, now that she was finally leaving. She knew her aunt didn't really have any place for her. And she knew her mother wasn't going to show up. So she had decided on Andrew and his buddy as a place to live to begin with. She would see how that worked out. He was funny. And she liked him. Maybe he was the best of all. She had sent him a message that she would meet him and his buddy at their cabin. He had sent her the address and a little map. She would be there that afternoon if she could get a ride. She knew he would be waiting for her.

While she was waiting in the library, she knew people were watching her. She decided not to try to get another message to Andrew because she was nervous enough already. Somebody could find out she was the one who had been using the computer. Maybe send her to jail. And then there was the bigger problem. She still had to convince her aunt to take her where she wanted to go. It might be hard. Aunt Lily had said she was done with men. Forever. "They are worthless. The whole lot of them," she said. Who knows what she would say about Andrew. Or his buddy. Or the fishing shack. Or meeting him online. Or the others either.

Maybe she should ask her aunt to take her to Ashley's first, and then find a way to get a ride from there. She didn't think Ashley would have a car. But she had to do something. And now she had to wait longer in the hot library. She looked around for books for a while, but couldn't find anything that started off fast enough. It was too hot to read. Besides she wouldn't be able to finish it before she left. She put her head down on her arms and dozed and then slept. When she woke up, Jenny was shaking her shoulder. Sticking out her tongue at her. Still wouldn't speak. Pointed like a clown towards the office.

When she got to the office, her aunt was signing papers. Aunt Lily gave her a hug, and after she said *Sorry Sorry* a few more times, asked what Angelique had done to get into so much trouble that morning. Angelique just shook her head and kept quiet. Her aunt asked the woman if that was it. The woman nodded and went to another room to make copies. She gave her aunt copies of what she had signed. Then it was over. The woman shook Angelique's hand as if she were an adult, then shook her aunt's hand and said goodbye. Goodbye to everything she hated. Andrew and his buddy were waiting for her down the road and that made Angelique smile.

Her aunt threw a blanket aside and put Angelique's bag and cardboard box carefully in the back seat of the old white Cadillac, the car her aunt kept saying she was going to get rid of because it used too much gas. The Cadillac was the one thing her aunt had gotten in the divorce. The house had gone to her ex-husband because she couldn't afford mortgages. Her aunt had always liked the Cadillac. She said it made her feel elegant. It reminded her of the days before the gun. Angelique wanted to try one more time to say goodbye to Jenny so she asked her aunt to walk back to the cottage with her, but when they got to the cottage, Jenny wasn't there.

Twelve

Once they were moving down the road, her aunt asked if she wanted to stop to get something to eat before she dropped her off at her father's house. The shriek was so loud her aunt slammed on the brakes.

"What?" her aunt screamed back. She moved the car to the side of Route 18. Angelique looked at her. Her aunt asked, "What?" again.

"My birthday. My eighteenth birthday. Did you even remember? I do not live with my fucking father! I will never live with my father! Done with him! Why do you think I asked *you* to come? Besides I have people. People waiting for me."

"Don't you ever curse at me young lady. How was I supposed to know where to take you?"

Angelique breathed in. Took in air. Let it out. They had taught her to do that when she was mad.

"So what? What now?" her aunt asked. "What people? Are you going to live with another family?"

"Not exactly."

"Well, what exactly?"

"I'm going to live with my boyfriend. He loves me. He's going to marry me."

"What boyfriend?" Her aunt could really yell when she wanted to.

"His name is Andrew. He lives on the lake. Twenty-two miles from here. It's on your way home. You can just drop me off there on your way back home. It's easy to find. Just off the highway. I found it on the map."

She had thought about how to say this part. She had thought it sounded good. But her aunt hadn't stopped there. Her aunt had to ask how she knew this boy. She had thought about that answer too. She wouldn't be able to give much of an answer except one she made up. Her aunt sure wasn't going to understand online dating sites. She was too old for that. So Angelique said that he was the brother of one of the girls in her cottage. It wasn't true. But it sounded better than meeting him online. And that she'd never actually met him in person.

Her aunt made a sound in her throat. Maybe she had learned that breathing thing too. But then her aunt went on for a while about men. And love and marriage. "And what about birth control. You don't have any pills do you. I know you probably don't. And boys aren't ever responsible. If they were there wouldn't be so many single mothers. You are not going anywhere. You will be staying with me tonight until we figure things out."

They drove for a while. It was quiet. The air conditioning had cooled the car. The road was smooth and straight, running along the edge of cornfields. Then her aunt said, "We should eat."

Thirteen

S he turned into Hamburger Haven at the crossroads. When she pulled into the parking lot, there was a thump. Her aunt jumped.

"What!" she yelled again.

The sound seemed to have come from behind them. "Maybe it's the spare tire in the trunk." Something shifted a little. Then they both screamed. It was something in the back seat. Moving. The blanket moved. Then nothing moved. They got out of the front seat and opened both doors to the back seat. Pulled on the blanket. A hump. Moving. Shoes. A girl. Jenny.

"What!" again. "What in the world!"

"Did you think you could get away with sneaking her out? On top of everything else. What were you thinking?" Her aunt had met Jenny. She knew Jenny was her roommate. Leave it to Jenny to mess this up for her.

"Me? What did I have to do with it?"

"She didn't. It was me. I was the one who hid me," Jenny finally said.

"Lordy, Lordy. I don't like surprises." Her aunt talked funny sometimes. "Jenny's a runaway. They will be coming to get me. You have to go back. Right now!" her aunt said right to Jenny's face.

As if Jenny would walk herself back down the highway and decide to go get herself locked up again. And Jenny. Jenny was crying. And mad. Fists about to fly. Looking at Jenny, she could hardly believe what was happening. Nothing was going like it was supposed to. And anyway it was still her birthday. Not that anybody had thought about that.

Andrew though, he had thought about her birthday. He had said he had a birthday present for her. He had made a bracelet box for her out of wood from a hazel alder tree. But the way things had been going, she might never see it. Or have a boyfriend. She thought about just walking the twenty miles herself. Or hitchhiking. But Jenny was crying and her aunt's voice was getting louder. Angelique began shouting that there was no way she was turning around.

A truck driver who had just gotten out of his truck was walking over to see if there was a problem. By this time both girls were crying and screaming, but her aunt shook her head when he asked if something was wrong. "Just teenagers," she replied. He said to let him know if he could do anything, that he had teenage girls of his own. Then he turned to walk into the restaurant. In a lower voice, her aunt told Jenny to stop it right now. Told both girls they were going to go inside and sit down at a table, order a hamburger, and talk about this.

"I can't go back. I can't go back. I just want to see my boyfriend," Jenny sobbed while they waited for the hamburgers.

"What is it with you girls and your boyfriends? Your mother was sixteen when she had you Angelique. True love. Love of her life. That was your father. And look how well that turned out. Every one of her babies had a different father. And where is she now. Jenny you have a lifetime for boyfriends. So eat. You are going back. I cannot, cannot, do you hear me, be responsible for a runaway. They will put me in jail. So here's what's going to happen. We are going to eat and then turn the Cadillac around and drive back so Jenny is not missing overnight."

Fourteen

The words *No No No No No* came out of Angelique's mouth in a stream, louder than she meant. Her whole body tensed and her face got red.

"It might not be your fault, but you got me into this. However it happened we are going to find the simplest way out. Now. That's it. That's the end of it." Her aunt's soft brown eyes glared hard. At both of them. Angelique hadn't usually thought of her aunt taking charge of anything, but she had.

"I know you think I forgot your birthday but I would never do that," her aunt said more softly. She handed her a birthday present. It was heavy, like a book, wrapped in paper with a cake and candles on it and curly ribbon. When she tore the paper off she found a Stephen King book. She was thinking horror. She loved horror movies. But the book was called *11/22/63*. History. The assassination of President Kennedy. Not horror. Her aunt said it might keep her out of trouble for a while. The book was huge. She would never finish it. It didn't seem like a very good present. But while Jenny continued to sniffle, her aunt told her about the book, that she couldn't put it down it was such a good story. A man ran a diner. But if he went down the stairs in the back of the diner he could go back in time to 1958. He could buy hamburger for his diner for what it cost in 1958. So he kept going back. But then he found out he could also change the story. He could keep things from happening. After a while he figured he could do something big. He could change history. The biggest thing he could think of was to keep the president from being killed.

"So does he?" Angelique asked.

"It's complicated. And why would I tell you that? That's what they call a spoiler. You read it. Think about something besides a boyfriend for a while."

After they finished eating, Angelique got up from the table and her aunt asked where she thought she was going.

"Can't I even go to the restroom before we turn around?"

Angelique had one thing in mind. The restroom was next to the door to the kitchen. She slipped through the swinging door and headed for the back door of the kitchen. She had seen the trucker who had spoken to them in the parking lot leaving after his meal to head back to his truck. She caught up with him and told him she was desperate, that she didn't want to fight with her aunt, that her aunt's problem was with the other girl. She had just gotten caught in the middle.

He asked her how old she was and gave her a long look when she said eighteen. Then said he had kids of his own and that had seemed like a wallop of a fight. He could maybe understand she needed a break. He would take her to her friend's house for the night, but that he wanted to meet her friend and be sure they were going to have her stay. He wasn't going to leave her out on the side of the road. She knew it would have to be Ashley's house until she could figure out a way to get to the cabin, but at least she was out. She quickly grabbed her bag from the backseat of the Cadillac, threw the book in, and left the cardboard box. He opened the door for her and she jumped up into the cab. The sun was lower in the sky as they drove down Highway 18. The trucker told her about his last trip and about each of his three kids, all mostly grown now. He seemed happy to have a chance to talk about them.

Fifteen

She really wanted Andrew that night, not Ashley with her baby. She didn't want to babysit anybody's baby, but for one night she could do it. Maybe two. Ashley had a phone. Or maybe she could buy her own phone. She could go anywhere from there. She felt pretty good about that. Nobody was going to chase her anymore. Or lock her up. Or tell her they had a plan. But there was no point in being out if she couldn't get to where she wanted to go. She imagined Andrew was wondering about her, where she was. For a minute, she still felt like a runner, even though she knew she wasn't.

And then they were at Ashley's house with the Lovely Louise Love Spells sign out in front. There was no car in the driveway lined with maple trees. The window shades were pulled. As he had promised, the trucker went to the door with her. She had always been afraid of Ashley's mother, Louise, who looked a little wild. She wasn't so sure Ashley was right about her mother's powers being a scam. And Angelique was pretty sure from Ashley's emails that Louise wasn't going to be happy about her being there, so she hoped no car in the driveway meant Louise wasn't home.

It was Ashley who opened the door when she knocked. She smiled. "What are you doing here? I thought you were going to go live with some boyfriend." Ashley gave her a hug. She liked it when people really hugged her. Hugged her like it mattered.

"You look the same as before you went away."

Angelique heard crying in the background. "It's the baby. Hungry or something all the time."

After Angelique introduced Ashley to him, the trucker said, "Well, I'll get your bag and then be on my way, but you let your aunt know where you are."

Sixteen

After they settled in the living room, she with Ashley feeding the baby a bottle, Angelique wanted to know from Ashley what it was like to have a baby.

"I was screaming and cursing. I told them to get that thing out of me. I wanted them to cut me open and get it out. Her out. After they did, my side hurt. I was sore for a long time. But I can get into my bikini again. The scar isn't that bad."

She wanted to know why Ashley decided to have a baby.

"It just happened. I was on the pill and then I couldn't get free pills anymore. The clinic stopped doing that. But my boyfriend didn't. And I couldn't kill a baby. And besides, she's a little me."

Angelique wanted to know what Ashley's boyfriend was like.

"Ex you mean. Sexy of course. Older than me. Tall. He was nineteen. He left before the baby came. Said he was going to North Dakota where everybody gets jobs because they have oil or something up there. He got into a fight. Got arrested and never came back."

She asked where Ashley had met her new boyfriend. She told her it was when she went to church with her mother. And Ashley wanted to know where Angelique had met this boyfriend she was going to see, if she had met him when she was locked up. Ashley told her those boys were messed up. She told Ashley she met this one online. Ashley wanted to know what he was like. She told Ashley she had seen him from his photo online. He was blonde and handsome and tall. She was going to get a ride to the cabin on the lake where he and his buddy lived.

"Angelique, you haven't actually met him? He could be a rapist or a murderer. You hear those stories all the time. What do you think you're doing? You don't really know anything about him."

She told Ashley she sounded just like her aunt and the Old Bag. She said she knew Andrew was fine. He came from the Community. That she had fallen in love with his picture. And he had made her a bracelet box out of hazel alder for her birthday.

"You don't know that. He could just be saying that. He could be lying about everything. That might not even be his picture. He could be an old bald man."

Angelique said Andrew had decided he didn't want to be baptized, and so he was not going back to the church.

"He loves me. He wants to marry me. And I'm pretty sure he isn't old or bald."

Seventeen

In the morning when the baby woke up, Ashley's mother yelled at her to get the child out of bed and change her. While she did, Angelique asked Ashley if her mother knew about her. Angelique had slept on the floor next to the crib. Ashley said she had told her, and her mother had agreed it was an emergency, but a one-time emergency.

While Ashley was feeding the baby they sat together in the living room, and she asked Ashley about the boy across the street she could see from the living room window. He was standing in the driveway throwing a basketball through the hoop over and over again.

"He's strange. But he's nice. His mother isn't. She's just plain crazy. He plays basketball at the high school. It's his last year. You should hear his story. He's like you. He was gone for a year, except he was kidnapped. Everybody says now that it was his real dad that took him, but it was a long time ago. Nobody knew where he was. I think he was seven or eight. I guess that's what made his mother crazy."

Angelique went out the front door and across the street to meet the boy. His name was Daniel. He was practicing free throws. Toeing a line painted on the driveway every time. There didn't seem to be any other kids around, probably because houses were small in the neighborhood. Houses were built after the war. Two bedrooms and one bathroom. A lot of older people lived in them, a couple from as far back as after the war. The one Ashley lived in had belonged to Ashley's grandmother, the second Lovely Louise.

Angelique stood there for a moment, looking up at Daniel. He was tall and skinny. He had a nice smile. When she asked if he had brothers or sisters, Daniel told her between bounces of the ball on the concrete that he was an only child. He got his name from his mom, Daniella. She couldn't have any more kids after him. He told her his mom was always afraid something was going to happen to him. His mom was pretty young when he was born. About like Ashley and her baby, except that he had been a premature baby. And then he was gone for a year, so now everything was like that for his mom--about to be a catastrophe. He said he thought his mom was probably watching out the kitchen window to see what he was doing right then.

She asked if he had really had his picture on a milk carton. Daniel said Ashley told everybody that. He thought Ashley worried sometimes that some-body was going to steal her baby since it happened across the street from her house. But it had happened a long time ago, Daniel said. He was kidnapped when he was seven years old. And the man was a stranger but he turned out not to be a stranger to his mother. Angelique sat down on the step beside the driveway.

He went on bouncing the ball and shooting. She wanted to know how they grabbed him. Daniel said it wasn't like that. When he was walking home from school, a man called out to him. The man knew his name and knew his father's name. The man said his father wanted him to get a chance to go to the carnival in town. They would meet up with his father at the carnival. And ride the Ferris wheel. And drink Lemon Shake-ups. Eat elephant ears. And yes, he knew now that he shouldn't have gotten in the car. But the man knew his father and the carnival sounded pretty good at the time. He remembers getting on the Ferris wheel that day and a pony ride. Corn dog. Lemon Shake-ups. His father never showed up at the carnival. After a while he got really tired. The man told him he could lie down in the back seat and rest until his father came. Looking back, he thought the Lemon Shake-up was probably drugged. He had quit drinking them after that.

When he had woken up it was morning. The most confusing thing was the carnival was all there. They were setting up rides, but it was in a place he had never seen before, at the edge of a town. The man had been watching him wake up. His father wasn't there. Or his mother. But he wouldn't ever forget how the whole carnival just popped up. Like a kid's pop-up book. Out of nowhere. Somewhere he didn't recognize. He hadn't known where he was. He had kept asking everybody where he was. They had told him he was in Shady Creek. They all had told him the same thing, so he had started to believe it. The man had said to call him Uncle Pete. He had thought that meant Uncle Pete was a brother to somebody in his family. His mother. His father. Or maybe he was a great uncle. He remembered crying for a while. Then he had gotten mad and told Uncle Pete to take him home. Right then.

But he wouldn't. He had told Daniel the carnival would just be there for a few more days. All the kids would be disappointed if they didn't get to go on the rides. And since he was with Uncle Pete, he would get to ride the pony whenever he wanted. Then they would get him home. But they hadn't. He had cried every night before he went to sleep. He had prayed the way his mother had taught him. He remembered having a sick feeling in his stomach. Not being hungry. People trying to get him to eat. Wanting his parents to come and get him. Not understanding why they didn't come. After almost a year of the carnival at the county and state fairs and in Florida in the winter, his father showed up one day. Punched Uncle Pete. Uncle Pete had said it was his kid and he had a right. "Not now. Not ever." His father had yelled and punched Uncle Pete again and had taken him by the hand and led him off the carnival lot. No police. No handcuffs for Uncle Pete. His father had taken him home. Said they would never speak of this again. Home had seemed a lot like it was before he left. But not his mother.

Eighteen

Angelique told Daniel about how the police had come for her and for her sister. She remembered one of the times they had come in the middle of the night to take her and her sister away from their mother. Her mother had been screaming and holding on to her and her sister. Angelique's wrist had hurt for a couple of days after. She had thought about it a lot for a while. She had known her mother and the boyfriend were probably drunk. The police had put her and her sister into a car in the backseat and buckled them in without a car seat. The car had glass between the back and the front seat. They hadn't turned the siren on. She had cried. For her sister, it was more like bawling when she was never going to stop. Kept saying *Mama*. Her sister had dropped a baby doll somewhere around the trailer steps when they took her out, and she wanted it back. She had named the doll Miranda June--who knew why? The house the police had taken them to had been warm. The bed was soft. The woman there had been so worried about her and her sister. She had had nightgowns for them. Like she was expecting them. And for a long time it had been better than their mama's.

Daniel made every free throw shot. He said the line painted on the driveway was exactly the right distance. Same as a real court. When he missed one, he told her "seventy eight in a row" and came to sit beside her on the step. He asked if he could touch her hair. He said he hadn't seen anything like it. His own was so straight and brown. She nodded. He touched the curls beside her left ear. He said it felt like a cloud of wire. She laughed. "A cloud could not be made of wire."

He heard his mother calling his name and shouted "Yeah Ma, seventy-eight in a row." He knew that's not what his mother wanted from him because she didn't care about basketball. He stood up and leaned against the side of the house throwing a shadow across her. He told her his mother didn't want him to go out with girls. Didn't want him to play basketball. But he had tried out and made the team three years ago. This would be his senior year. He told her the story of how he made the team. His mother had home schooled him until high school. By the time he was fifteen he had grown to six feet three. His mother hated that he wanted to try out for the basketball team so much that she had tried to sabotage the tryout. The night before, he had come down with what he thought was a stomach flu but it wasn't the flu. It was food poisoning, and not an accidental case. It came from a sandwich his mother had made. His usual double turkey sandwich lunch that his mother made for him had had a couple of long expired slices of turkey stuck next to the cheese.

Daniel admitted to Angelique that he didn't just eat food--he inhaled it. Ever since being on the road with the carnival. It's the way they all ate. So he didn't taste anything different. The next day he had been able to muscle through the stomach pains and weakness. The tryout was sad. Very sad. He couldn't hit anything. But his coach gave him a pass. Coach had an instinct that he could be good. And he was taller than most. The only way he found out about what made him sick was when his mother was mad at his father. She had been having nightmares again like the year he was gone. She would cry out "They stole my baby, stole my baby, my baby!" When she started having the same nightmares again, Daniel's father tried to calm her down. She got really mad about the basketball. In the middle of crying one night she told her husband she had tried to stop Daniel from trying out for the team. Daniel still wasn't sure why his father had ever told him the story.

"Hey, Milk Carton Kid. What are you doing with my friend?" Ashley hollered. The baby on her hip started crying. She wouldn't have heard much if he had answered. Angelique started to wander back across the yard. The basketball dribble started up again and the thump when it went through the hoop and hit the pavement.

She asked Ashley why she didn't like Daniel. Ashley told her it wasn't Daniel. It was his crazy mother. His mother was raised in Alabama. And her father, Daniel's grandfather, had been a preacher in one of those churches where they were baptized in the river. They talked silliness. Words that didn't make any sense. About like out of Penelope Ann's mouth. And snakes. And no sex. No drinking. So she had gotten married to Daniel's father the day after high school graduation. She was pregnant or not depending on who you asked. Daniel was born seven months later. Some said premature. But she had always been sure something would happen to Daniel. Like she felt guilty about something. And when he was kidnapped, she went crazy. She never was the same after that. Everybody said so. She tried to keep him from playing basketball. Who poisons a kid's food? And then she wanted to be sure no girl ever got near Daniel. Ashley said sometimes she had felt like flashing her breasts in that direction when she was nursing the baby, just to make her mad.

Nineteen

That night things went okay. She stayed with Penelope Ann, as she had promised, while Ashley went out to the only movie in town with her new boyfriend. The baby went to sleep. Ashley was out late. Ashley's mother was also gone, working the second shift at the factory. She curled up with a pillow on the floor next to the crib in Ashley's room. She went back to her book. Her aunt had been right. It was a page turner. The diner owner was dying and he wanted somebody else to take over changing the story. It would be a big thing. An important thing. To stop a shooting. When it was the president. She fell asleep reading but didn't hear Ashley come in. She woke up in the morning when the baby did.

That's when the trouble started. Ashley was feeding the baby. She and Ashley were eating some leftover cold pizza for breakfast. She had stayed her two nights, and she should have been thinking about how to get twenty miles down the road to see Andrew. But that sound of the basketball thumping on the pavement had started again. The sounds stayed in her head. She didn't think it was just coincidence that Daniel was out there practicing free throws so early. The sound was reminding her of how much she liked Daniel. For a while she forgot about Andrew. She knew that it probably wouldn't work out to stay here with Ashley. And Daniel didn't have a place of his own. He was still in high school. But she liked listening to the story of how he had been away all that time and lived through it. She liked that about him.

By the time Ashley's mother left for work, Angelique still hadn't decided how to get to the cabin on the lake. She saw Daniel's mother leave in the car.

She thought she would just wander across the yard and maybe he would sit on the steps with her again for a while. Talk to her. And he did. After a while when Daniel said maybe she could meet him down at the Dairy Queen that night, she said yes. He said his mother wouldn't like it if they walked there together, but they could meet later. It wasn't that far to walk. So she stayed with Ashley and played with the baby the rest of the afternoon. She washed her hair and sat in the sun and brushed it while the curls dried. She put on her tightest pair of shorts and borrowed some eye shadow and lip gloss from Ashley. She sat with Ashley and played some more with the baby while she waited for it to get dark.

Twenty

"One night!" Louise kept repeating. "I told her only one more night. Already one kid and a baby. Two bedrooms. What do people expect around here from me? Where am I supposed to put my clients? Now if you would get busy and start learning the business, things could be different."

She was just getting out of the shower and could hear the screaming. Louise had thrown Angelique's clothes, her bag, and her book out onto the lawn to make her point. Angelique asked Ashley to bring her something from the lawn to put on, but Ashley had her hands full with the baby. Like always. So she wrapped a towel around herself and went out to pick up something to put on. Daniel was not out practicing. But his mother came out of the front door and yelled across the street, "Where I come from that's what people call a slut."

She started to wonder what Daniel's mother knew about the night before. Maybe nothing. How could the woman know what went on every second of the day with her son? Or night. Had she followed them to the park? He had brought a blanket. They had laid on it to look at the stars. After a while they pulled the blanket over them, and she took all of her clothes off. The wet grass felt nice on her back. Daniel felt good on top of her. Inside of her. Not something his mother needed to know. Whatever Daniel's mother knew or didn't, it was time to get out of there. Between her and Louise it was time to go. She put on clothes, shoes. Took her bag outside and threw things in it. Money. Where was her money? She was picking up clothes and shaking them. Frantic. Then she found her money in the pocket of her other shorts. Her book had landed on the wet grass with pages down. Ashley came out and said, "Sorry." People seemed to say that a lot to her. She kissed the baby. She wasn't quite sure why she did that. She said goodbye to Ashley. Hugged her. Started walking towards Route 18, towards Andrew and the cabin. No sign of Daniel. She would have liked to have seen him instead of his wicked mother. Right now she was more in love with Daniel. But his mother was scary.

Going right on Route 18 took her through the middle of town. She needed a phone. A smart phone. For the internet. She stopped at the store with a sign on the door that said *Free Phones*. She asked to see the smart phones. She wanted to be able to get online again. She picked out a phone case with rhinestones and said, "That too." The salesman was about her age. He was short and wore glasses. He flirted with her a little. Asked if she already had a phone number she wanted transferred. She told him no. He started filling out a form with her name. She gave her aunt's address. Then he asked for her social security number. She told him she didn't have one. Or maybe she did. But she didn't know the number. He asked about a bank account. Or a credit card. "Why would I need a bank account?" she asked. "It says right there on the sign on the door that the phone is free. I know I have to pay for minutes. I have cash." She pulled out bills from her pocket to show him. He explained that the phone would be free if she signed a contract. To have a contract, people would have to be able to check her credit history. "What people?" she asked. "It says *free phone*. And I have money to pay anyway." He asked her some more questions but couldn't come up with answers that fit his form. He said she could go over to Wal-Mart and get a prepaid phone that had some minutes and she could call people. "Internet?" she asked. He shook his head. After she yelled at him to screw himself and his free phone, she started walking faster toward the edge of town.

She was shaking a little she was so mad. She should have eaten something. And she wasn't taking pills anymore. Maybe that's why she felt shaky. She was mad at just about everybody now. Daniel didn't even bother to come after her. Free phone guy could have helped her. Lovely Louise. Daniel's mother. Her own mother. Where was she anyway? She picked up the pace. She had become a good power walker while she was locked up. After a while she saw a sign going the other way that showed she had walked four miles. Even at a twenty minute mile, she figured she could make it before it got dark. The shoulder of the road was dusty. Not much traffic. An old man stopped and offered her a ride. She wasn't so sure about him. She shook her head and kept walking. At a small store with one gas pump, she stopped to buy Band-Aids for her foot that was bleeding. They didn't sell Band-Aids but the man behind the counter found several for her anyway. A blister on her heel had broken open. She drank for a long time from the water fountain. She bought a bottle of Gatorade to take with her. Her teacher had given her one when they had walked together. She wished she had somebody to walk with her now. The time would go faster. Back on the road the sun had gone under a cloud. The breeze was cooler. It stayed that way until she found the cabin hours later.

Twenty One

It was right at the corner of the highway the way the map from Andrew said it would be. Ashley had been wrong about what he would be like. Andrew was blonde and blue-eyed. Tall. Glad to see her. She was falling in love at first sight. His friend was David. The cabin was more like a shack. There was a For Sale sign in front that looked like it had been there for years. She saw a dock with the boards coming loose. Old fishing poles. One big room. A picture window onto the lake. A table. A refrigerator that had rusted. Bunk beds with old chenille bedspreads. It wasn't much but it wasn't that bad they told her. Except when it rained. The roof needed work. Maybe they would fix the roof since they were not paying the owner rent. Since he didn't know he had renters. Andrew said they knew how to fix the roof. They just needed to find shingles and a ladder. They had some tools they had brought with them.

That evening they fried fish for her. A rusty iron skillet. A red-eyed bass they had caught earlier. Fish and bread from the old Wonder Bread day-old outlet down the road that still sold bread, just not Wonder Bread anymore, they told her. Beer they had traded two bass for. They told her they were lucky. They grew up together on farms next to each other. They happened to be the same age. This was their time to explore. They weren't shy about telling her that meant touching flesh. It meant sex. Breasts. Trying things. It was so much easier for them than men a long time ago, they said. All they had to do was meet women on the internet. It was too easy.

Andrew told her he had had a sweetheart for a couple of years. Charity. A beautiful girl who braided her long blonde hair every morning. He hadn't been able to kiss her. Or hold her hand. Or touch her at all. She believed in all the rules. Believed in the church. But she was sweet. She had told him he was her true love. The only one on earth. Andrew wasn't so sure that there was only one possible true love ever for him. He looked at David when he said it.

Andrew had in fact already decided he would never go back to the church. David either. But they hadn't told their parents. Or the other elders. There had been three girls before her in the cabin. They didn't have a car but they did have one smart phone they shared. It's how they got online to find the girls. They were both handsome. They had shaved off their beards. They shaved every morning. They had taken photos with the phone of each other and put them online. The girls all seemed to find the cabin with no trouble.

After they ate, Andrew presented her with the bracelet box he had made for her. She didn't have any bracelets to put in it, but she loved the box. She kept running her hand over the wood along the grain. It was beautiful smooth wood. Polished. The felt lining was red, just like he had said it would be. She asked if all the girls got a bracelet box. Andrew explained he had only made one, and it was for her. They had been calling her Birthday Girl. He said she was the only one they knew who had been planning to spend her birthday with them.

Twenty Two

N ow she was sure she was in love. No one had ever made her anything like this before. With the beer at dinner and all of the walking, she was tired and really sleepy. She thought this was the most happy she had ever been. This was exactly the way her life was supposed to be. They give her a bottom bunk. She crawled in and before she turned towards the wall, Andrew kissed her forehead and lay down on the narrow mattress beside her with his clothes on. "First night for cuddling," he told her. She could feel his erection against the back of her thigh, but almost as soon as he lay down beside her she drifted into sleep.

The next day she sat on the dock in the sun and fished with them. They showed her how to hit a three pound bass in the head with a rock to kill it. How to gut it on the old wooden picnic table outside the cabin. Cut its head off. Filet it with a sharp knife. Scale it. She walked to the store and bought more cornmeal, oil, fresh tomatoes, a 2 gallon can of peaches, peanut butter, and dish detergent with a little of the money she had. That night, after they cooked the fish and ate it, David sat out on the dock fishing again as the sun went down. Andrew gently undressed her and went to bed with her in the small bunk without his clothes on, their bodies melding into the last light from the sunset.

The next afternoon while Andrew was fishing on the dock, Angelique and David were inside washing up dishes. David wanted to kiss her. He whispered to her that it was his turn, and he knew Andrew wouldn't mind. She was surprised, but he leaned over and kissed her gently. Then again, harder on her mouth. And she let him. It turned out both Andrew and David wanted to have sex with her, but not at the same time. That seemed okay with her. They had filled a kitchen cupboard with condoms the colors of the rainbow. And black. They always asked her what color next. David was rougher with her than Andrew. Slapped her a little. Wanted things Andrew didn't. Would forget to kiss her. Andrew told her each day that he loved her. She was sure Andrew was going to propose to her.

On the days it rained she went back to reading her book, playing around with one or the other of them, moving cans to catch water that dripped through the roof. Once it rained for two days and soaked one of the mattresses before the sun came out. They emptied the cans of water. Dragged the mattress and bedspread out into the sun on the dock to dry. That afternoon, David came back with the news that he had found shingles for the roof. They could have the leftovers from a crew working on a house a mile away. The crew was from their area, most of them older. They had built half the new houses along the lake. The shingles were too heavy to haul by hand. The crew was going to drop them off at the end of the day. They would leave them some nails. Let them borrow a ladder. They would start the next day. They wanted to do something to the cabin to pay for staying there. To surprise the owner. Even if they had decided they were not going back to the church, they were honorable men, they told her, more than once. She loved them. She was in love with them. What she also loved was not being locked up. She loved nobody else knowing where she was living. No police. No judge. And nobody telling her what to do. She would marry Andrew and live with them both forever.

Twenty Three

Three things happened to change her mind. The first thing was David. One afternoon David asked her to walk up to the outlet to get some bread. David had his hand on Andrew's shoulder when he said it. When she reminded them they already had half a loaf of bread, David said, "Go anyway." She looked sideways at Andrew. He nodded and told her this was their time to explore. To try everything. "It's okay," he told her. "Come back in a while.

The second thing was Charity. Charity showed up by herself in a buggy one afternoon. Angelique was out on the fishing dock sunning herself in a new lavender bikini she had bought when she had walked all the way to Wal-Mart on the other side of town that morning. Andrew had taken off his tee shirt and was on the roof hammering shingles. It was a small cabin, and they had almost finished the roof. David had gone to trade bass they had caught earlier for beer. They both thought the bass run was about done for that year. When Andrew came down the ladder from the roof and wiped sweat off with his shirt, the first thing Charity asked was, "Who's she?" Charity pointed at her.

"A friend of David's," Andrew told Charity. And it went on from there. Charity told Andrew that she was hurt that he hadn't come back to see her. That it was not forbidden to come back to see a sweetheart. That she loved him more than life itself. Charity said her papa wanted to know when Andrew was coming back to be baptized. Andrew tried to take Charity's hand but she pulled it away. Tears were running down Charity's cheeks. When she looked up at Charity from the dock, Angelique thought she looked like a china figurine. Long skirt. Laced boots. The kind of figurine her mother used to keep on the shelf in the living room before one of her boyfriends shot at each one of them one night when he was drunk. David had come back with the beer and stood at the end of the dock just watching. Angelique was frozen in place. Both she and David could see Charity biting her lip, but the tears kept coming. Angelique wished she had a shirt or a towel to cover up with. David shook his head at Andrew. He was trying to tell him something.

The lip biting and the tears turned into sobbing. It was like watching a movie in slow motion. Charity turned and walked back towards the buggy. Swayed a little. David stepped backwards and said her name. Charity didn't say anything. She started walking slowly past the dock towards the buggy and the horse. David turned to Andrew and said to him, "You shouldn't have told her. I told you not to. You can't let her drive the buggy all the way back by herself. You know that." David offered to take Charity back. She didn't speak but she moved over to make room for him on the bench. He took the reins from her hand.

Twenty Four

S o first David. Then Charity. Third was Andrew. She confronted him and asked why he had said she was David's girlfriend. He said it just happened in the moment. He called her Birthday Girl the way he had when she had first gotten there. "But I came here because of you. I love you." she said. "Whoa" he said to her. "Like I told Charity, I am not going back to the church. Not going to be baptized. I am never going to get married."

Angelique told him that everybody got married and had kids. It's what people did. He told her marrying wasn't what he was cut out for. He and David planned to stick together for a while. Maybe with girls, maybe not. He told her she had already been at the cabin longer than the other girls. She could stay a while longer if she wanted, but he hoped she wasn't going to be a baby about leaving. Angelique decided she was not going to let him see her cry. Not after Charity. Everybody left her sooner or later anyway. Or threw her out. It was not the first time.

She didn't really know how to swim, but she headed back down the dock and jumped into the lake for the first time. Let her head go under, and the water go up her nose. She discovered she could stand up. She walked out a little further until the water was up to her chest. She felt mud oozing under her feet. And something sharp that cut into her foot. They had been telling her to watch out for the zebra mussel shells that were sharp as glass.

A lot of things were starting to bother her. Her aunt had always tried to tell her, "Life is messy. It's complicated." Her aunt had said if Angelique would remember that, she would be happier. But her aunt didn't seem all that happy. Maybe Andrew hadn't lied, but it felt like it to her. She shook her head hard to get some of the water out of her hair and out of one of her ears that was stopped up. She was mad. At him. At David. At everybody. She started to wade back. When she pulled herself up the ladder and out of the water she followed Andrew and said "Give me that phone for a minute." She logged into Facebook.

Twenty Five

When she took the phone from Andrew, she logged in as herself and wrote messages to three of the men she had first met on Facebook: Chuck, Brian and another man named Jacob. To each one she said she would be waiting on the lakefront public beach in town for him to come and pick her up. He would know her from her lavender bikini. She was so mad she didn't care who it was. Whoever came first. But she didn't tell any of them that. She wanted to be sure somebody would come. Then she went in to throw on a shirt and put her clothes in her bag again. She stuck the rest of her money in the pocket of her shirt, put her shoes on and walked out the door slamming it behind her, almost pulling the door off its hinges.

By the time she had walked the mile to the beach the sun was beating down. The beach was crowded with little kids. She sat down next to one who was building a sand castle. It was a girl with a sun hat that had sunglasses sewn into the hat. Weird little kid. The girl was using the bucket to make a mold and dump it upside down. The sand was too dry to stick together so it kept falling apart. The little girl's mother was busy texting on her phone. She just sat for a while watching the girl who must have been three or four. After two more tries where the sand fell apart, she leaned over and told the little girl to go fill the bucket half full with water from the lake and bring it back. She showed her how to fill the rest of the bucket up with sand. The little girl started to tip it to make a mold again, but she stopped her. She showed her how to drip the sand out with her hands one drip at a time to make a drip drop castle that would stick together. Her own mother had shown her once a long time ago. A few minutes later, a shadow fell across her and the little girl. She looked up.

"Well girl," he said to her, "Are you ready to take that trip to Disney World? I got plenty of money. I just need some company."

He picked up her bag. Pulled her up with his hand. Gave her a hug and put his arm around her to lead her to his truck. She waved to the little girl with the drip drop castle. He was Chuck. He was a lot older than Andrew or David. She remembered from his profile he was almost thirty. He had a beard, shaved head, and sunglasses. She climbed up in his truck like she had been doing that all along. The truck had big tires and was sitting up high. So was she.

He had gotten there quickly, so she thought he must not live too far away from the lake. He took the back road from behind the new Wal-Mart. She knew that direction was north. But then he made so many turns she didn't know where she was. Or where he was going. She tried to pay attention to how to find Route 18. She thought she needed to keep track of that. She didn't like not knowing. The trip only took a few minutes. Turns onto gravel roads. Then smaller dirt roads. He talked to her about growing plants. Said he had been doing it since he was twelve. She talked to him about fishing. The last turn was deep into the woods.

"Well, this is it," he said as he stopped the truck. He helped her down from the truck. It was a big step.

Twenty Six

His place was an old cottage. She didn't know what was different about this place. Something. Either creepy or like a fairy tale. Three big German shepherds came running up. They almost knocked her over. He told her they were friendly. Not to worry. She began to think a place that far back in the woods could be bad. Maybe he was the one she shouldn't have gone with. He showed her the house. Said she could have her own bedroom if she wanted. She didn't know what to say. He put her bag down in the living room. The house was old and the things in it were old. The bathtub had claw feet like the one in her grandmother's house. The kitchen had an old sink but a new refrigerator.

He asked her if she wanted something to eat. She remembered she hadn't eaten anything all day and nodded. He said he was going to cook an omelet. Cracked eggs. Beat them. Poured in some milk. Cut up mushrooms and put them in the pan to cook. She didn't want to tell him she hated mushrooms so she just kept quiet. He cut up something he called basil and put it in. He set plates and silverware on a small table covered with oilcloth. Two chairs. When they settled down to eat she couldn't remember anything tasting that good. Even with mushrooms. They seemed to be a different kind. Ones she had never seen before. Afterwards she picked up a towel to dry the dishes he was washing. She set them on the table since she didn't know where to put them. After a few minutes she moved behind him and put her arms around him as he finished at the sink. He had more muscles than Andrew. He turned around and kissed her. She kissed him back. He led her into his bedroom. Later her bag followed. And stayed there until they left for Florida.

The next morning as they lay in bed, she looked closer at his tattoos in the sunlight and told him she liked them. They were different. She touched the tattoo on his left arm and asked what kind of bird it was. He told her it was a raven. She said she had always wanted a tattoo. He told her the trick to this one was that it was done by a woman in Amsterdam, where he bought his seeds. Angelique said she wanted the first one to be a wasp on her neck like the girl with the dragon tattoo. And then angel wings for her name. A snake. She stopped, realizing she might be asking for a lot. He told her to start small and see how she liked it, that the wasp on her neck would be a good one because it would be small. He said he knew a woman in the southern part of the state who could do it. He would take her there when they drove down to Florida. He was waiting for the plants to finish drying. She asked why Florida. "They pay a premium price. And they know quality. Not like here."

For several weeks they lived like this. He cooked for her. Things she didn't usually eat. She wiped the dishes when he washed them. They walked in the woods with the dogs. They went into town shopping. He went off to work on plants. She read. When he came back in the evening he gave her wine that tasted better than the beer at the cabin. He told her about the different kinds of seeds he grew. They explored each other's bodies. She had never really touched a man's nipples. He stimulated her body in different places. He didn't even mention condoms.

Twenty Seven

When he left her in the afternoons to go to check on his plants, he would tell her plants don't water themselves. He didn't ask her to come with him. She knew that he went out the back and down a set of stairs behind the house. The stairs went to a door that pulled up like a cellar door. It was an old door with most of the paint peeled off. Almost like the diner in her book. The book was long, and she was a slow reader. She had started to wonder about time travel. It seemed so real in her story.

One day when it was really hot, he left the door open. She wanted to know where he went. She walked over to the opening and peeked down the stairs. He saw her staring into the huge underground concrete block room. He told her to come down the stairs. She was afraid he would be mad. Instead he started telling her that he knew she liked to talk. Talked a lot sometimes. And he liked listening to her. But she could never talk about this. He was serious. She nodded her head. Her red curls fell forward over her face that had turned red too.

He told her this place had been a fallout shelter built in the fifties by an Amish man with a big family. The man wanted to be sure the whole family wasn't wiped out when the bomb was dropped. When there wasn't a bomb, people forgot about it after a lot of years. They quit coming back to the cottage in the woods because it wasn't good farmland. The woods were too deep. He told her the cottage was covered with vines when he bought it at auction. A buddy of his had known about the old fallout shelter and told him it might be what he was looking for.

The brightness of the lights and the green of the plants startled her. He had lights strung everywhere. On wires that were hanging like white Christmas lights. She wanted to know why he watered the plants every day. She had only ever seen things growing in the fields. He said these plants didn't grow like the ones in the fields. He put plant food in the water. It was all about the water and the light. He said his parents were old hippies from the sixties. He had been growing his own plants since he was twelve. He told her some people around there did grow plants outside. But his grew bigger and quicker this way. The seeds were the best you could get on the planet. It's why the people in Florida asked for him. And he was always careful. She shouldn't worry. He had never been caught. He showed her where he had plants just beginning to grow. Some budding. A lot drying. After a while they went back up the stairs together.

Twenty Eight

He started to tell her about the trip. How it would be. They would leave on a Monday. She told him she had never been anywhere. How her mother had left and gone to another state. Nobody knew where. Maybe to Nashville. Her mother and her sister, but not her. Everybody else just stayed here. Lived here. Her father. Her aunt. Her grandparents. Nobody else ever left the state.

He told her Disney was magic. Castles. The Eiffel Tower. Whatever she wanted it to be. Except for the tattoo, they would drive straight through. He didn't like to stop overnight with product in the truck. He would drink a lot of caffeine and drive until he got the delivery made. Then they could do whatever she wanted in Orlando. He had a buddy who would come and water plants for him while they were gone. Feed the dogs. He told her Florida was going to be hot and humid so be prepared. He took her to buy some more shorts, another bikini at Wal-Mart. Sunglasses. Sunscreen. A pair of sandals.

She said she wanted to dye her hair black. He groaned. A redheaded beauty, he called her. He loved redheads. Why would she want to get rid of that beautiful hair he wanted to know? She told him she needed things to be different. So he bought her the hair coloring. Two boxes. One didn't seem enough for all that hair. That night he helped her put the color on. Afterwards she looked at herself in the mirror with the hairdryer in her hand. The black was harsh. The difference shocked her. A different person she decided.

On the Monday they were to leave, he spent the whole morning packing the shipment. He had a particular way, he told her. There were a lot of small packages. By the afternoon, it was time to leave. He told her he had done this hundreds of times. "And nothing goes wrong. But it always pays to have insurance. That's why nothing goes wrong."

He handed her a roll of bills that she stuffed way down in the pocket of her shorts. He gave her a prepaid cell phone from Wal-Mart and said he would call her on that phone if he needed to. He put a pistol in the glove box and asked her if she could shoot. She nodded. "Well don't," he said. "You won't need to."

As he backed the truck out of the driveway, he said it would be about three hours before they got to the tattoo artist. He called her that. A tattoo artist. After a while, she asked if the woman was one of his exes. He told her she had a strange way of thinking about that word, "ex." Almost any boy who had flirted with her. Or kissed her. Or she talked to online. She had a list of men she talked about that she called exes. He said most of them probably weren't really exes. He only had one of those. An ex-wife from a long time ago. He said his policy was love the one you're with. And no he hadn't hooked up with the tattoo artist if that's what she was asking. Then she wanted to know about his ex-wife. The only thing he would say about her was that he loved her. That his wife left him because she didn't like the business. And she got tired of the woods.

She asked about the needles. She was worried about how much it would hurt. And shouldn't she get drunk first. That's what people always told her.

"You listen to people a lot. People don't know much sometimes. You don't want to get drunk unless you want to bleed a lot."

Twenty Nine

Roxy had her own place. It was in the middle of nowhere. One big room. Designs all over one wall. She was the only one working there. It was quiet. No one else was around. Roxy looked like she could handle anything just by the way she stood with her hand on one hip. Chuck had told her they were coming. They started talking about a couple they knew who had left their farm to go live on a sailboat in the Bahamas. To her, it sounded like they had known each other forever. She turned away from them and started looking hard at the designs, but Roxy had one already picked out for her. It was exactly what she had hoped for.

She argued with Roxy who wanted to put it on her shoulder not her neck. She came close to tears when Roxy completely said no. "Your shoulder has muscle, not your neck. It would hurt like hell if I put it on your neck. Besides, it would never heal because you move your neck around all the time. I know you want people to see it. And they will. I will put it up high on your shoulder near your neck. It's not like you are going to be buttoned up like a nun. I can see you're not that type. Wouldn't be with Chuck if you were."

That made some kind of sense so she settled for the shoulder. At the end Roxy held another mirror up. She could see how perfect the small wasp was. Roxy asked for her fee in product. Said it was the best anywhere. And they got back on the road. Angelique told him she loved it and the needle wasn't bad. Not as bad as she thought it would be.

Thirty

Two days later she looked at herself in the mirror in the Days Inn in Orlando. Her black hair was sticking out in different directions. Her face was pale next to the black hair. She knew she looked terrible. She hadn't slept for two nights. She kept twisting around to try to see the tattoo. She had been washing it and putting the ointment on that Roxy gave her. But she couldn't exactly see it. Chuck could have looked to be sure it was okay. But he had been gone since Tuesday when they got here. And nothing. Nothing. Nothing. He said he would be back in an hour. Maybe a little more. Then they would go see the Eiffel tower. And the lights when it started to get dark. And fireworks.

The phone in the room kept ringing every few minutes. Not the cell phone she walked around with in her hand and wouldn't put down. She knew they were calling her to see when she was going to check out of the room. But she kept waiting. The truck was still in the parking lot. Locked. She was positive he was coming back. He had gone off with somebody to deliver the product when they got there on Tuesday. Probably to get his money. He had checked her into the room and told her to take a nap. When she woke up in the afternoon, he wasn't there.

She had had a knot in her stomach since then. She had stayed up during the night and flipped between news channels. Looking for drug busts. Or something. On Wednesday, nothing. He had booked the room for two nights so she had stayed. Kept the door locked. Jumped when there was a knock and a woman shouted, "Housekeeping." She told her to go away and sat on the edge of the bed watching the news. She held onto the cell phone. Her stomach felt worse. She thought she should eat something. She took the plastic key card he had given her. She walked across the street to a MacDonald's and ate a hamburger and french fries. Kept looking around at people. Then came back and threw up.

On Thursday she could believe that the phone in the room was going to keep ringing until she did something. She didn't want to do anything. She wanted this awful day to be over. Another night had gone by and the cell phone hadn't rung. Angelique finally had fallen into an exhausted sleep around 3:00 in the morning with her fingers wrapped around the phone. She woke tangled in the sheets from a dream where Chuck was pointing a gun at two men bigger than he was. The dream was so real she was sure it had actually happened. The sun was bright through the gap in the curtains, and she knew it was time to get up and figure out what to do next. Still no calls had come from the cell phone that had fallen on the floor during the night. Maybe he had lost the number. She felt sick again and started to wonder why her period was so late. It was hard to count back through the days over the last few weeks. Just thinking about it made her feel worse.

Thirty One

Angelique jumped when she heard the sharp knock on the door. She hoped it was Chuck, but she knew he had a key. The knock turned into pounding. She waited. More pounding. "Open up. I know you are in there. I just need to talk to you for a minute." It wasn't housekeeping. It was a loud man's voice. She knew she didn't have a choice since he was going to keep pounding until she unlocked the door so she opened it a few inches.

"Your time's up. It's two hours past check-out time. It says so right on the back of the door there. We need to get this room cleaned. We can just put your bag in the office until you are ready to go." The man's name was Rickie pinned on his shirt. She remembered him from the front desk. Angelique couldn't get words out. She felt the tears hot on her cheeks. She was mad at herself. She didn't want to be the one who cried all the time when something went wrong.

"Look sweetheart, he's not coming back. That truck's been parked out front since you got here. If he were comin' for you he woulda been here by now. I don't think he meant to leave you. You're a pretty little thing. Maybe I could take you to get something to eat when I get off my shift." Angelique was furious now. She didn't want anybody calling her sweetheart. She didn't like the way Rickie looked at her. "You don't know anything," she spat out.

"Well here's what I do know. Your key doesn't work anymore. Either come up to the office and pay to stay or get out. Fine with me either way. If you don't leave I can always call the cops. They might bring those sniffing dogs. Might be real interested in checking out that truck that's been sitting there. Or maybe you want to get into that truck and drive it back home. I can help you get the locksmith we use here to make you a key."

She wasn't about to admit to him she didn't know how to drive. "I'll pay for tonight," was all she said, and she followed him to the office.

Thirty Two

After another sleepless night, Angelique wasn't going to wait for anybody to bang on her door and throw her out. She still had clean clothes and decided on a shower, then counting her money. She had four hundred thirty-seven dollars left with some change. Chuck had told her about emergencies. He always sounded like he knew what he was doing. So why was she here, and he wasn't. Everything he had told her about Disney World seemed so stupid now. She had some money, but if she had to go on her own she wanted to get into the truck to get the gun in the glove box. She started looking around the room for something that would break the glass in the window. But when she thought about it, she knew he had that gun with him. She knew it from the dream.

She decided to go to the office on her own this time. There was a woman at the desk instead of Rickie. She asked about internet, and the woman pointed to the computer at the end of the room. The men she had met online all lived a long ways away from Florida. She decided to leave Ashley a message on Facebook. She knew Ashley had a cousin who lived somewhere in Florida. She thought Ashley would probably tell her to call her father instead. But Ashley had always had parents. She didn't know what it was like. She left Ashley a message that she was stuck in Florida waiting for Chuck to come back and asked about where in Florida her cousin lived. Then she asked Ashley to have Louise cast a spell over Chuck to make him love her and come back to her. She finished with *answer me now*.

She figured she would wait around a few minutes to see if Ashley picked up the message on her phone. The woman at the desk asked her if she needed anything and said she looked pale. Angelique shook her head. The woman seemed nice. She asked her if she were a runaway. Angelique shook her head again and told her that she was eighteen and could do what she wanted. The woman said "Sometimes that's harder than running away. We get runaways here sometimes. It's warm all year. The ones that always wanted to go to Florida. Disney World. So where are you headed?"

"Um, maybe to my friend's cousin to wait for my boyfriend. He hasn't called me yet."

"And isn't that an old story," the woman said.

"No I think something happened to him. He left his truck here."

"Now that is peculiar," the woman said. "How long has it been?"

When Angelique told her, the woman said "He's probably gotten himself into some trouble and isn't coming back. Where does your friend's cousin live?"

"She's sending me her address," and Angelique walked back over to the computer and logged on again. Ashley had been right there and had given her an address for her cousin Cynthia Ann in Fort Myers, but Ashley also said she should call her father instead. Or his girl friend. And Ashley told her the spell would work better if Angelique would come and see her mother in person. And she wasn't sure it would make Chuck show up at a certain time. Angelique shook her head. Then she asked the woman at the desk about Fort Myers.

"Oh honey, that's all the way down the coast. Right now you are in the middle of a big state. But I can tell you how to get to the bus station if you want to go. It isn't far."

Thirty Three

Angelique ached for Chuck. His rough beard. His blue eyes. She was sure she loved him more than she had ever loved anybody. She just wanted him to call. To come back. She was tired already of this place where the sweat dripped off of her as soon as she stepped outside of the cold air conditioning. She could see the heat shimmering off of the palm trees. And no breeze. But if she left Florida and the phone she held in her hand rang, she would be too far away to meet him. She decided to go to see Ashley's cousin Cynthia Ann in Fort Myers. At least it was in Florida. And the woman had said it was on the coast. Maybe Cynthia Ann lived near the beach. Before she left the hotel, she wanted to use the computer in the lobby again. The woman at the front desk asked her if she had had anything to eat since she looked so pale. Angelique shook her head. She had felt sick since she had gotten up. The woman offered to make her some toast. She seemed so nice Angelique thought she should eat the toast.

Then she went back to the computer. She had wanted Ashley's mother to cast a spell to make Chuck love her and come back. So she started another message to Ashley that began *I really need this*. She told Ashley that she didn't have a way to pay her mother online, but she would pay her when she came back. And Ashley asked right away when she thought that might be?

She heard someone come into the room with heavy boots and looked up. She saw the woman at the desk nod her head slightly in Angelique's direction. The man in work boots stood at the desk talking and Angelique went back to

Facebook. Ashley was telling her again that what her mother did wasn't magic. She couldn't make people appear. And besides, Chuck would have come back at least for his truck by now if he could. She told Angelique she thought that dude must be in a lot of trouble. Or dead.

Angelique messaged back, "Look, just ask her about the spell. You know she is good at it."

Ashley asked if she knew when Chuck's birthday was, but Angelique didn't know.

Ashley said her mother was working first shift at the factory but would be home later and she would ask her then. She finished with *"You know she's not going to like it. You should get your ass back here."*

Angelique told her she was going to find Cynthia Ann so she could stay close to where Chuck would be when he came back. Ashley replied that she was dumb to stay in Florida. She also let her know that Cynthia Ann was a little crazy.

Thirty Four

When she was getting the directions to the bus station, the woman told her that she would probably have to go to Tampa first and then figure out how to get to Fort Myers since the Greyhound bus didn't go directly there. Angelique wondered what else could go wrong. She was just tired of it all, of everything being so hard. But the man with the boots said, "Well wait a minute, I am headed to Cape Coral right next to Fort Myers. I could get you there this afternoon. It's about three hours." The woman said, "Isn't that lucky for you? Maybe your luck is changing. Must be in the stars."

At the end of the conversation, Rickie came in through the door behind the desk to start his shift. Angelique remembered why she hadn't liked him. Right away he said, "Wanda, are you at it again? What are you doing to her? She's just a scared kid. And here you are taking advantage." He turned to Angelique. "You know what she's trying to do, don't you?"

Angelique was still mad at the way Rickie had looked at her and had called her *sweetheart*. He had even threatened to call the cops about Chuck's truck. All she wanted was to get out of the hotel. Get away from these people and find a place to wait for Chuck to call her. She had his phone on vibrate in her pocket but still no call. She glared at Rickie and shook her head a little. She took another look at the man with boots and said "Okay, I'm ready to go now if you are."

"You idiot," Rickie said, and "At your own peril."

The man told her his name was Boots, had been since he had been a kid with big feet and had worn big boots. He picked up her bag and headed towards the door while she followed. The heat and humidity and the bright sunlight hit her as she walked out the door. "You look a little wobbly," he said to her. "I've got water in the truck for you."

For the first hour as they left Orlando he told her stories about when he was a baseball player in spring training, trying to break into the majors. He told her he could swing a bat and knock it out of the park, but they kept trying to teach him not to always swing at the first pitch. He said he just saw that ball coming and his body reacted every time. The coaches kept trying to tell him to take a look at the different pitches a pitcher was throwing and pick the one he wanted before he swung. But he couldn't keep from swinging right away. He was a switch hitter. Either side of the plate, and plenty good either way. They liked that. A homerun hitter. But they kept telling him not to swing first. Then they told him he only got three strikes, like that was news. And they tried to tell him a lot of different ways. But he would just see that ball coming at him, and the bat would come around. The stories made her laugh. He seemed nice, this man Boots. He asked her if she wanted something to eat and what she liked. She realized her stomach had been growling, and she was hungry. When she said waffles he found a Waffle House. After that she listened to him a little while and then dozed. When she woke the sun was lower in the sky, and they were closer to Cape Coral. He asked her about the address. She read him the address from where she had written it on her hand. She told him it was the cousin of her best friend, but the cousin was a little crazy according to Ashley.

"You know, Angelique, that's way out the other way past Cape Coral, and crazy might not be what you need right now. I was just thinking. I own a little apartment building, just six apartments all furnished nice. Girls about your age live there. Just one girl in each apartment. One of the girls left the other day to go back to Tampa to take care of her sick grandmother. Maybe you would like to stay there just for a few days. I bet Chuck will call you in a day or so anyway, and then he will pick you up."

Thirty Five

"Does it have internet? Your apartment?"

"I said furnished, didn't I? Well how could anybody live without internet these days."

Angelique just nodded. She felt more tired than she had for a while and just wanted somewhere to sleep. The apartment didn't sound so bad, and anyway she had never met Cynthia Ann and didn't know what 'a little crazy' might mean. At first the apartment looked like the perfect place to wait for Chuck. The building and the furniture were modern and seemed new. Boots brought her bag in, showed her food in the cupboards and freezer, left the key for her and told her he would see her in the morning. She put the phone next to the bed, took off her shoes, laid on top of the covers and slept for ten hours.

The next morning she signed on to her Facebook account and sent another message to Ashley asking if her mother had cast the spell for Chuck to come back to her. Ashley said her mother had been tired when she came home and had to work on her what her other clients needed. She said her mother kept saying *no jumping the line. Fourth generation and what use are you,* her mother had said. Ashley had told everybody a million times that she had no intention of doing what her mother did. Angelique asked again. "Tell her it's life or death" she wrote. "Chuck has to come back. And besides I think I might be pregnant."

"My mom is going to be so mad at you."

"Don't tell her. Just ask her again about the spell tonight, please."

She was drinking a glass of orange juice when she heard the doorbell ring. A girl with long dark hair who seemed about her age was at the door. "You the new girl?" she asked.

"Guess so. But only for a day or so." Angelique replied.

"Oh we all say that in the beginning."

"No, my boyfriend is coming to get me in a day or so."

"Well good for you I guess. I'm Brittany by the way. Boots asked me to show you around. You want to see the pool?" The pool was clear and blue surrounded by dwarf fruit trees in a courtyard. "You can swim and sunbathe out here most of the day. Dinner isn't until after seven. The clothes Boots wants you to wear for dinner are in the closet. There are a couple of different sizes. And shoes."

"What do you mean dinner?"

"Oh it will just be with an old friend of Boots. He will come and take you out to a nice restaurant for dinner. They are all gentleman. The first time it's probably Howard. He won't even touch you. Just wants to look at your breasts."

Thirty Six

Months later, when Angelique was at the doctor's office for the ultrasound that told her the baby would be a boy, she thought back to that hot and humid day in Orlando, and she remembered how her life had changed: the morning sickness that she had hoped might be a feeling of missing Chuck, the slight nod of the woman at the desk to Boots who took her to Cape Coral, and the spell she had asked for from the Lovely Louise.

Now, of course, she knew what Rickie had meant. Wanda and Boots had been looking for girls like her. And she still felt stupid about that. But it had been a place to stay for a while, even a place with a swimming pool. She had liked lying out in the sun. And Boots and his friends hadn't seemed all that bad. They had taken her to nice places for dinner. Had liked her breasts that were getting bigger. They had been gentlemen. Wanted to look at her. Made her feel like one of those women Chuck had talked about who sat in the windows in Amsterdam.

Lovely Louise, who had been known all over the state for casting the spell that brought the Hollywood actor back to his high school sweetheart, had not been able to make Chuck reappear. But she had sent her cousin Cynthia to find Angelique after the first week with Boots. Cynthia was one of them, the spell casters in the family. And Angelique had settled in with Cynthia, craziness and all, to wait for Chuck. But now it seemed she was waiting for a baby instead.

Angelique was sure that this baby would have blue eyes. Chuck's blue eyes and hers, of course. Her mother's eyes like blue-eyed grass. She was ninety-nine percent certain this baby would have blue eyes. But the condom had broken once with David when he was rough with her. And there had been that one night with Daniel. She wondered if she would ever see Daniel again. Or her mother. Or her sister. Or Chuck, who had never come back. Maybe Ashley was right, he might even be dead. But she hadn't seen him in her dreams as dead. Just fighting with some other men with guns. Not that any of it mattered now. It was just her. And Cynthia Ann. And the baby boy coming in three more months.

Afterward

Angelique's story continues every week as a serial with episodes posted on **Serealities.** Readers are invited to vote on what happens next in Angelique's life. Vote to change the story at www.serealities.com.

About the Author

Linda Casebeer lives in Birmingham, Alabama and on Lake Manitou in Rochester, Indiana. She is married to Edwin Casebeer, writer and professor emeritus. She is a cofounder of Serealities, an online new fiction site where stories are published weekly in a serial format and readers vote on what happens next in the story. She has also written *The Last Eclipsed Moon,* poems published by Cherry Grove Collections.

www.ingramcontent.com/pod-product-compliance
Lightning Source LLC
Chambersburg PA
CBHW070350130626
46556CB00007B/3111